Praise fo

"The Pikes Peak region is filled with natural beauty, but too often we overlook the people that inhabit the region—especially people who have been marginalized or forgotten. Lucy's book reminds us of the richness, the power, and the impact of the contributions by black people that have called this area home. The Pikes Peak region is stunning—not only because of the mountains, but because of the people who have given it spirit, life, and art. Lucy's book reminds us that black is indeed beautiful!"

**—Mike Edmonds, Vice President of Student Life/
Dean of Students at Colorado College**

"I can't imagine anyone better than Lucy Bell to reconstruct Colorado Springs in the 1940s and tell the story of Oliver Bell, a young black boy facing discrimination and segregation. Relying on her background as an educator and historian, Lucy has exhaustively researched the era through living histories, manuscripts and period photos. Lucy is a skilled storyteller and writer able to weave together compelling anecdotes of her beloved Oliver's life with factual details of Colorado Springs as it existed at the time. I have eagerly awaited this book."

**—Bill Vogrin, writer and journalist.
"Side Streets" columnist for**
Colorado Springs Gazette.

"In a book destined to become a classic, author Lucy Bell has opened a window on Colorado Springs' colorful history that will delight readers young and old. Enhanced by the sensitively rendered illustrations of Linda Martin, COMING UP traces the coming-of-age experiences of Oliver Bell in the early 1940s. With pages full of mischievous boyhood adventures, unexpected consequences, and ever watchful neighbors; each chapter has a surprise ending, historic photos of the actual people in the chapter and fascinating information about relevant topics of the day. From the hidden tunnels under Saint Francis hospital to the untold secrets of an era when courageous citizens fought the scourge of the KKK, COMING UP is a tribute to Colorado Springs' hard-working families who came to the city to give their children a chance at life in schools that welcomed all of them. Vivid, poignant, and always thought-provoking, COMING UP is a treasure."

—Kathleen F. Esmiol*

*Additional note from author Lucy Bell: Fannie Mae Duncan, legendary Colorado Springs entrepreneur, whose father-in-law and other acquaintances are characters in *Coming Up*, found an advocate when she met Kay Esmiol. Kay based her 2013 book, *Everybody Welcome: A Memoir of Fannie Mae Duncan and the Cotton Club*, on years of personal interviews and tape recordings. Kay ensured that Duncan was inducted into the Colorado Women's Hall of Fame in 2012, but then her intention to honor Fannie Me took on an even bolder scope. After 24 years of dreaming, planning, fundraising and land acquisition, Duncan's life-size bronze statue, crafted by world-class sculptor Lori Kiplinger Pandy, will become reality. In the near future you can visit it in front of the Pikes Peak Center, at 190 South Cascade Avenue, not far from the Cotton Club's former location.

COMING UP

COMING UP
A Boy's Adventures in 1940s Colorado Springs

By Lucy Bell

Illustrated by Linda D. Martin

Lucy Bell

AMBIENT LIGHT PUBLISHERS

Ambient Light Publishers, LLC
PO Box 9105
Colorado Springs, CO 80932

Publisher's Cataloging-in-Publication data

Bell, Lucy, 1941-
    Coming up: A boy's adventures in 1940s Colorado Springs /
    Lucy Bell ; illustrated by Linda D. Martin
    p. cm.
  ISBN 978-0-9863324-3-2 (pbk.)
    1. Bell, Lucy, 1941- 2. Martin, Linda D., 1961-, ill. 3. Juvenile
Fiction - Readers - Chapter Books 4. Juvenile Fiction - Historical
- United States - 20th Century 5. Juvenile Fiction - Historical -
United States - Colorado 7. Juvenile Fiction - People & Places
- African American 8. Juvenile Fiction - Biographical - United
States
    PZ7.1.B455 Co 2018
    813.'6

                                                    2018952766
  ISBN 978-0-9863324-5-6 (pbk)

For the historic black community of Colorado Springs
whose courageous spirit lives on
in every act of racial justice.

TABLE OF CONTENTS

INTRODUCTION

The stories in this book all really happened. They were told to the author by her husband, Oliver Bell, who was born in Colorado Springs in 1933. Ollie attended Helen Hunt Elementary School, South Junior High, and graduated from Colorado Springs High School.

Except for the public schools, Colorado Springs was a segregated city when Ollie grew up. Although circumstances were sometimes difficult, Ollie had fond memories of his boyhood.

He graduated from the University of Northern Colorado where he was an outstanding athlete in baseball, football, and track. He taught physical education in Colorado Springs School District #11 for thirty years. Oliver died in 2002 at the age of sixty-nine. He loved telling these stories and would be very happy to know that you are going to read them.

COLORADO SPRINGS LOCATION MAP

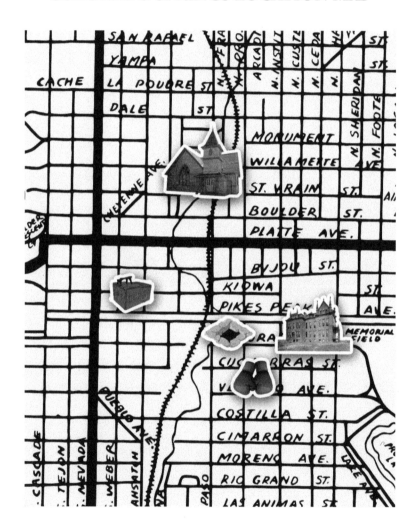

MAP KEY

CHAPTER ONE: THE KNOCKOUT PUNCH
712 East Cucharras Street

CHAPTER TWO: WATCH OUT FOR HAINTS!
St. Francis Hospital
825 East Pikes Peak Avenue

CHAPTER THREE: THE SECRET
HIDEOUT
Pikes Peak Avenue and Prospect Street

CHAPTER FOUR: ROCK OF AGES
People's Methodist Church
527 East St. Vrain Street

CHAPTER FIVE: YOKUM IN THE DARK
Green Parrot Shining Parlor
214 East Pikes Peak Avenue

CHAPTER 1

THE KNOCKOUT PUNCH

Colorado Springs, Colorado
July, 1941

"Dem bones, Dem bones gonna walk around
Now hear the word of the Lord."

Shucks, Grandma, Oliver thought, you done played that song five times already this morning. Grandma sure did love her Delta Rhythm Boys gospel records.

Oliver had to admit he liked the songs, too, although thinking about bones walking around gave him chills down the back of his neck. Skeletons and haints and such was something he'd just as soon do without.

Boy was out on the porch snapping at the flies before they got stuck on the yellow, speckled flypaper that curled down from the rafter. Oliver loved that old dog, gimpy leg and all. He went outside to join him and sat down on the top step.

"Sit down in the shade with me, fella." Boy limped over and rested his nose on Oliver's leg.

Oliver could see the top of Pikes Peak between the trees and St. Francis Hospital across the street. He pulled up his socks to cover his skinny ankles. Pants too short again. He hoped Grandma would get him some new ones before school started so the other second-graders wouldn't call him "Highwaters."

Just then Oliver saw his two buddies coming down the street. Sammy led the way with Billy trailing behind. They joined Oliver by the big cottonwood tree that shaded the front yard.

Oliver swatted a fly that flew slowly past his nose and greeted his friends, "Sure is hot."

"Hot, alright," Oliver's friend, Billy, agreed. He took his cap off and fanned his face. His blonde hair was plastered to his head from the heat.

Oliver smiled at him. What a good pal. Oliver didn't have a bike of his own, but he could always ride Billy's. Didn't even have to ask. If it was leaning against the side of Billy's house, it meant nobody was using it, and he could just take it and ride.

Sammy picked up a stick and scratched his name in the dirt. "Hot, and boring, and nothin' to do. Cain't even play Cowboys and Indians no more."

Billy looked surprised. "Why not? I liked the way the Heckle's goat pulled the covered wagon."

"Yeah," Oliver remembered. "Fun to ride in, even if it only fit one. No, it wasn't the goat. Courtney Heckle spoiled it."

"What did he do?" Billy asked.

Oliver sighed. "Well, you know Courtney always want to be the Indian?"

"Cuz he got the bow and arrow," Sammy added. "What make it so bad, he taught all the girls in the neighborhood how to sharpen sticks into arrows."

Billy frowned. "It's no fun dodging those arrows. One of these days he might hit something. Was it his big supply of arrows that spoiled it?"

"No, worse than that." Oliver explained, "All us cowboys got an idea how we could fix Courtney. We built us a fort."

Sammy grinned. "A big fort out of tumbleweeds. Higher than our heads and full of stickers. We all hiding inside the fort, peeking out through the tumbleweeds, when we saw him coming down the street with his bow and arrows."

"But Courtney. . . man, oh man!" Oliver shook his head.

"What?" Billy asked. "What did he do?"

"He took off running for home. We still inside the fort laughing 'bout how we scared him. But here he come back again, holding a rag soaked in kerosene. He wrapped that rag around his arrow, put it in the bow, and set a match to it."

Billy's mouth dropped open.

"He shot a flaming arrow into our fort," Sammy said. "Those tumbleweeds started catchin' fire, and everybody skedaddled, but Grandpa

Duncan sitting on his porch saw us running. He jump outta his chair, lay his pipe down, and yell, 'Hey, you pie-face apes! You startin' fires over there?'"

Billy said, "When he calls you pie-face apes, you know your mama gonna hear about it."

Oliver nodded. "He called Grandma right after he called the neighbors to come put the fire out."

"Did you get a whipping?" Billy asked.

Oliver and Sammy both nodded. "And Grandma say that's the last Cowboys and Indians she ever want to hear about."

The boys looked up when they heard somebody whistling. Oliver's teenage cousin, Sonny, sauntered past with his lanky, long-legged walk. Sonny was the top athlete in the neighborhood. He played center on the Boys Club basketball team. He was even learning how to golf with Billy's dad's clubs.

"Hey, Sonny."

"Hey, guys." Sonny kept walking. "Guess you don't know what Frank got," he called over his shoulder.

Sonny's big brother, Frank, the only black runner on the Colorado College track team, had such good grades in high school he'd been awarded a scholarship.

"What, what's he got?" Sammy asked, skipping ahead to keep up with Sonny.

"Got boxing gloves, that's what. Three pair."

Oliver remembered hearing that Frank competed in boxing at the college when he wasn't running track.

"We want to see 'em!" The boys crowded around Sonny as they headed toward his house.

Oliver had listened to the boxing match on the radio last spring, and everybody cheered when the announcer yelled, "Louis has K.O.'d Buddy Baer in Round Six!"

"Are they Joe Louis gloves?" he asked.

"See for yourself," Sonny answered as they reached his house.

The boys took their caps off as they went in the door.

"Mornin, Aunt Hattie," Oliver said.

"Mornin, Miz Bell," Billy and Sammy echoed.

Aunt Hattie tucked her hair behind her scarf as she greeted the boys.

"How's your mother and grandmother, Oliver?"

"Fine, Aunt Hattie."

"And how are all the Browns?" she asked looking at Sammy.

"Just fine, Ma'am."

"And your family?" She nodded to Billy.

"Just fine, Miz Hattie."

"Billy, I'd like for you to tell your daddy how much we appreciate him lending his golf clubs to Sonny. It's a funny sport to me, but he enjoys it." Billy nodded, as Aunt Hattie continued.

"'Spect you came over here to see what Frank brought home. He's at the store right now, but Sonny, you can take them to Frank's room."

The boys smiled, and shoved their caps back on their heads. They hurried to Frank's room, and there on his dresser they spotted them—the boxing gloves.

"Wow!" Oliver said.

"They red!" Sammy exclaimed. "I thought they'd be brown."

"Red, alright," Billy said, "with white laces! Can we try them on?"

Sonny hesitated. "We better wait for Frank. Ma, when is Frank coming home?"

"Here he come right now."

Oliver looked out the front door and watched Frank's blue Studebaker pull up in the driveway.

Frank came in, set the groceries on the table, and joined the boys waiting in the doorway of his bedroom.

"Sonny must have told you about the gloves. Well come on." He took the gloves from the dresser top.

"We'll see how they fit. But first of all you have to form your fist the right way. Curl your fingers down to the center of your hand and then put your thumb over the first two fingers."

Frank demonstrated, and the boys all copied.

After a few more practice times to get their fingers and thumb right, the boys stuck their hands out and got laced up. The leather smell of their hot hands inside the man-sized gloves floated in the air as the boys began to punch and jab.

"Hold it," Frank said. "Before you start punching, you got to get your stance."

Again, the boys watched and copied, and Frank nodded his approval.

"Okay," he said to Sonny. "You know something about boxing. Show them what you know."

Sonny threw a punch at Oliver. "Don't just stand there. Coulda knocked you out. You got to protect your jaw."

"This here's a jab." Sonny demonstrated on Billy. "Good duck, Billy."

"Protect yourself, Sammy. That one's called an uppercut."

The boys danced around throwing punches and jabs at each other.

Frank smiled. "We'll work on footwork next time."

By the next Saturday, Oliver heard that Sonny had rigged up a boxing ring in his backyard. He'd got ahold of four metal poles and looped clothesline rope around it.

Oliver told all his friends, and by ten o'clock Oliver, Billy, Sammy, Hansy, Jack, and Harold had all showed up at Sonny's backyard. Little Charles Edward came, too, even though he was only five and not old enough to box.

"OK," Frank said. "Sonny and I are the referees. We're going to match you up according to size."

Oliver and Sammy jumped up and stood back to back.

"You my size," Oliver said.

"You my size, too," Sammy answered.

Sonny shook his head. "No, Sammy. You're closer to Bump's size. Come here, Bump."

Harold, who was always called Bump because he had a big bump on his forehead, got up. He'd stopped by Sonny's earlier in the week for some lessons. "Do I get to do it? Watch out, Sammy, here I come."

Oliver sat down beside Billy in the cool grass as Sonny laced the gloves onto Bump, and Frank put another pair on Sammy.

"Go to your corners," Sonny instructed. "This will be a three-round bout."

Oliver looked around. He remembered hearing the bell when he listened to fights on the radio. "Where's the bell?"

Sonny hollered, "DING DING DING. That's the bell."

Hansy said, "I can do that, DING DING DING." Little Charles Edward jumped up and hollered, "I can do it, too. DING DING DING!" Pretty soon everybody was ding-dinging.

"All right, you guys. Quiet down," Frank said. "We're ready for the first match."

Oliver thought it was a great match. Bump and Sammy threw punches and jabs. They got into clinches six times, and Sonny had to separate them. Round two was short because Charles Edward started dinging too soon. By the middle of round three, Bump or Sammy never had really hit each other, but still it was fun to watch.

The July sun beat down. Oliver noticed Billy's face looking hot and red. "You want to move over in the shade?"

"Shoot no, we got a front row seat right here. I could use a drink, though."

"We better not bother Aunt Hattie. They's too many kids to be all going in the house after water."

"It's okay," Billy said. "Yowie! Lucky Bump ducked that time!"

DING DING DING. Round three was over. Sonny was standing between Bump and Sammy. Beads of sweat trickled down both boys' foreheads.

Sonny held up Sammy's left hand and Bump's right hand. "Folks, we got a split decision. It's a draw. Good boxing, boys."

Frank took the gloves off the fighters and looked at Oliver and Billy. "Your turn, fellas."

Oliver's heart was beating fast as Sonny laced the white laces of the red gloves over his hands. He looked at Billy who was getting laced up by Frank. Billy looked down at the ground.

"Go to your corners and come out at the sound of the bell," Sonny commanded. "DING DING DING."

Oliver bounced out—he was thinking about the fancy footwork Frank had taught him. Billy walked over to the middle of the ring like he was walking down the sidewalk. He must have forgot about the boxing way to walk. He didn't forget to defend his jaw, though. He had both gloves in front of his face.

Oliver kept bouncing. He kept his left hand in front of his face and took a little swing with his right. Billy brought his hands close to his face. All Oliver could see was the big red gloves. It was okay to punch him in the chest. Oliver gave a little swipe, but Billy stepped forward and swung at Oliver's jaw. Oliver stepped forward, too, and next thing he knew they were in a clinch. Sonny stepped in and separated them.

Oliver noticed Billy wasn't moving fast. Both of his hands were in front of his chest. His jaws weren't defended at all! Without even thinking about it, Oliver gave him a left to the jaw. Billy staggered backward a couple steps, and wham! Down he fell to the ground, flat on his back, the red gloves at his sides, his eyes shut.

Oliver stood petrified, his mouth hanging open. He didn't know whether to holler help or say sorry. He didn't think he'd hit Billy that hard. He didn't mean to hurt his best buddy.

"We got a knockout!" Sonny yelled, "A K.O. Right here in Colorado Springs. You saw it, folks. Right here in Round One. Oliver Bell has K.O.'d Billy Mudd! He is down for the count, one…two…three…"

Frank rushed over to Billy's side. "Shut up, Sonny!" he said. "Go in the house and get some water for Billy."

Frank knelt down and felt for a pulse in Billy's neck. Everything was stock-still quiet. A few blocks away a dog barked and a rattley, old truck's brakes squeaked on the Pikes Peak Avenue hill.

Oliver heard his heart pumping with a bump-bump-bump so loud he thought everybody must be hearing it. It seemed like forever, but in a few seconds, Frank leaned back with a sigh of relief and wiped the sweat from his forehead.

Billy opened his eyes, raised up on his elbows, and remembered where he was. He sat up straight, frowned at the silent boys staring down at him, and told them, "I wasn't knocked out. I was just tired."

Beginnings
The Sachs Scholarships for African American Students

Oliver and his friends always remembered the summer that they learned to box. When Oliver grew up, he boxed for twelve years, losing only one match during that time. While in the Marines, he won the West Coast light heavyweight championship. Other boys who learned to box that summer became boxers in high school or later, even little Charles Edward.

It all started when Cousin Frank brought the gloves home from Colorado College where he was a student. But how did that happen? In the 1940s, very few African Americans had the opportunity to attend any college, even if they were good students, and Colorado College was one of the most expensive private schools in the country.

It began with a man who got rich by investing in a popular invention—the Gillette Safety Razor. That man lived in Boston, and his name was Henry Sachs. His life was going well, but in 1900, he developed a cough that wouldn't go away. When he began coughing up blood, doctors gave him the bad news. He had tuberculosis.

This lung disease was hitting thousands of Americans. There was no known cure, but doctors on the East Coast recommended that patients go to the western states where clear, mountain air and sunshiny days seemed to help. Henry Sachs took this advice and settled in Colorado Springs with his chauffeur, James Jeffries, and housekeeper, Gertrude Lee. Between their care and the climate, Mr. Sachs recovered from this often fatal disease.

He was grateful to these two African American friends who had nursed him back to health, and he wanted to do something in return.

Being of Jewish heritage, he had encountered racial discrimination and believed that all people should have equal opportunities. He was looking for a way that he could help make this happen.

In 1931, Mr. Sachs attended the Colorado Springs High School graduation held at the City Auditorium. He was impressed with the speech given by Effie Stroud, who graduated at the top of her class. At the end of the ceremony, he went up to the platform to ask her about her college plans.

Effie's parents had come to Colorado Springs in 1911. Her father, K.D. Stroud, had been a pastor and teacher in Oklahoma, but the only job he could get in Colorado Springs was shoveling coal for the Rock Island Railroad in Roswell, five miles north of town. He walked to work every day, seven days a week, shoveling coal for seven cents per ton. He saved money for years and was able to start his own hauling business. He encouraged his twelve children to do well in school. They were all honor students, but there was no money to send any of them to college.

Effie told Mr. Sachs she would like to go to college, but she would need to work for at least two years in order to afford one year of college.

Mr. Sachs had found the answer he'd been looking for in his quest to contribute to racial justice. He offered to send Effie Stroud to Colorado College, all expenses paid, if she kept her grades up. Her success led him to establish a scholarship fund, and Oliver's cousin, Frank, was one of many who qualified to receive this opportunity.

Henry Sachs died in 1952, but the Sachs Foundation has continued to this day. About fifty new students receive scholarships to eighty different colleges around the country, every year. In its eighty-seven-year history, the Sachs Foundation has helped over 5,100 African American Colorado residents get a college education. Cousin Frank became Dr. Frank Elliott with a long and successful medical career in Denver.

Henry Sachs with Gertrude Lee and Jim Jeffries

Photo courtesy of Kay Esmiol and the Sachs Foundation

The real Aunt Hattie Bell and Cousin Frank Elliot

Photo courtesy of James Bell III

The real "Grandpa" Louis L. Duncan, buried in Evergreen Cemetery, Colorado Springs, CO. Louis Duncan was the father-in-law of Fannie Mae Duncan, who was married to his son, Ed.

Photos courtesy of Joe and Claudia Morgan

CHAPTER 2

WATCH OUT FOR HAINTS!

Colorado Springs, Colorado
July, 1942

A red, white and blue poster caught Oliver's eye as he hurried down the street after selling his last *Colorado Springs Evening Telegraph* at the corner of Pikes Peak and Tejon Streets. The white-bearded man on the poster scowled down at him and pointed a bony finger. Oliver read the words at the bottom: I WANT YOU FOR U.S. ARMY.

Oliver pointed his finger back at the man and said, "You don't want ME, Mister, but Grandma Creasey do, and I best be going."

From "Busy Corner" to St. Francis Hospital where Grandma Creasey washed dishes measured close to a mile. Oliver hurried along, but he slowed down when he came to the baseball field.

He heard the coach yelling at the players and he stopped to watch a group of white boys finish practice just as the sun slid down behind Pikes Peak. Oliver knew he'd be good at baseball if he had the chance. He could hit the ball a mile playing stickball in the alley with his friends.

He'd like to have a coach yell at him. He'd hit straight, run like lightning, and make that coach proud.

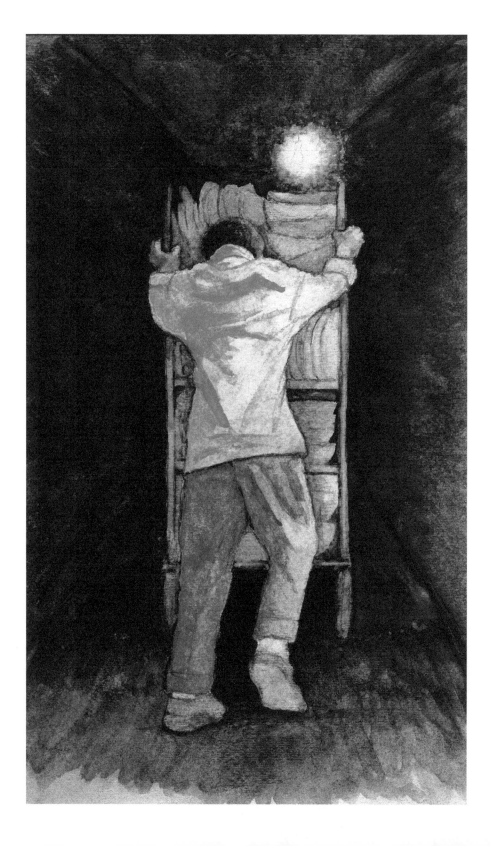

Oliver ran on and arrived at the hospital just as Sister Donatella swished out the door in her long, black habit. Black meant she was on the way to say her prayers in the chapel. During the day when she helped the patients, she wore her white outfit.

Oliver almost bumped into her in the doorway.

"Slow down, young man!" Sister Donatella ordered in her stern voice.

"Yes, Ma'am, sorry Ma'am," Oliver said, pulling off his baseball cap.

"Oh, Oliver, it's you," Sister Donatello said. "Are you helping your grandmother this evening?"

"Yes, Ma'am."

"That's good. There's a big load of dishes tonight. Six more TB patients came in yesterday."

She went on her way, and Oliver hustled down the dark hallway. Grandma said to be thankful for Sister Donatella. When Sister found out that their family with five children lived just across the street from the hospital, and only Mama working, she offered Grandma a job.

After the divorce, Daddy had gone back to Mississippi. He had another family now and couldn't help them pay the bills. Mama cleaned houses at the Broadmoor for $1.00 a day, and that didn't go far. Grandma moved into the little house behind Mama's house, and Oliver stayed with her, leaving Mama and his four sisters in the big house.

Oliver slipped into the kitchen where the stale odor of cooked cabbage lingered in the air. The water in the tall dishwashing machine hissed while it heated up, and Grandma Creasey leaned over the sink to scrape leftover food off the plates.

She turned when she heard Oliver come in and said with a frown, "Where you been, Boy?"

"Sorry, Grandma."

"Did you come straight here from the corner?"

"Yes," Oliver lied. Then he took it back. "No, stopped and watched baseball for a little while."

"Um-hmm. Thought so. Need to come when you s'posed to. Hear?"

"Yes, Grandma."

"Don't want me to get no switch now, do you?"

"No, Grandma." Grandma never did get the switch herself. She made whoever was getting the whipping go cut their own switch.

"All right," Grandma said. "Got most of these dishes ready. You can start loading."

Oliver slid the bottom shelf of the big machine forward and began to put the dishes into the rack. He had to stand on a chair to slide the top shelf out. He'd do that one later.

Steaming water sizzled and disappeared into the air. The water had to be boiling hot to kill the germs because all of these dishes would go back to the special diets kitchen. Special diets meant that these dishes came from the TB patients. TB stood for tuberculosis, a lung disease that people died from. Grandma said people with TB came to Colorado from all over the country because folks thought the mountain air might cure them, but lots of people died anyway.

Oliver knew that for sure. From the front porch of his house, he and his sisters could see the gurneys with covered-up bodies on them rolled out the back door of the hospital and loaded into vans.

Last week when his little sister Hazel saw the gurney, she said, "Look, look. Somebody going for a ride."

Jessie, two years older, reprimanded her. "Dummy! They not riding, they dead."

"They dead, and nobody even gonna ring the bell special for them," Mayme, Oliver's older sister, added sadly.

"Why not?" Jessie wanted to know. "I heard the bell ring special last week. Why they ring it then?"

"That's because Sister Mary Francis died," Mayme explained. "They only ring it special when one of the sisters dies."

Just as Mayme finished saying that, the big bell in the chapel began to chime. They looked at each other and counted out loud. " . . .ten, eleven, twelve." Twelve noon. Telling the time like it did every day. Nobody dead this time.

Oliver didn't like thinking about tolling bells and dead people. Instead, he daydreamed about playing baseball and hitting a home run.

Grandma interrupted his thoughts. "Oliver, I'll help you load the top shelf, and then I got to go. My leg been paining me all day. Cain't stand on it another minute. Got to go home, soak it, and get in the bed. You know how to load the clean dishes on the cart and take them to the kitchen. Can you do it by yourself this time?"

"Yes, Grandma," Oliver answered. "I can do it."

Oliver knew he could do it, but he didn't want to. The special diets kitchen was on the other side of the building, connected by a long dark tunnel. It was the very same tunnel that they wheeled the dead bodies through to get to the back of the building.

After Grandma left, Oliver sat down on the floor under the tall table waiting for the machine to finish the dishes. He tried not to think of dead people and ghosts, but the more he tried not to think about it, the more they popped into his head.

He remembered visiting Uncle George in Mississippi last summer. They were relaxing on Uncle's front porch in the cool night air. Uncle George sat in his rocking chair, and Oliver reclined on the bottom step, wiggling his bare toes in the dusty, red clay.

"Bout time for the haint to show up," Uncle said.

"Haint?" Oliver turned and looked up at his uncle. "What's a haint?"

"Well, a haint is somethin' that is, but it ain't. That's why they call it a haint. See that tall, skinny pine tree yonder? Watch over there and tell me what you see."

Oliver leaned forward, straining his eyes toward the piney woods, all dark and shadowy now.

All of a sudden, a shimmer of greenish light slithered toward the tallest, shaggiest pine tree. Oliver slowly stood up, and without taking his eyes off the light, backed his way up the steps until he stood behind Uncle George's chair.

"What's that?" Oliver whispered. "Is that the haint?"

"Reckon so. Come here every night 'bout this time. Never come further than that same skinny pine tree. They say an old Indian's buried under there, got separated from his spirit some kind of way. That spirit comes lookin' for him every night."

Uncle George slicked his hand over his bald head, leaned back and rocked. "Um-Hum. That's what they say."

CLANK! The dishwashing machine let out the noise that told it was done. Oliver jumped up so fast he knocked his head on the underside of the table.

"Dang!" Oliver swore, rubbing his head. "Them haints is out to get me for sure. Tunnel probably crawling with them."

He loaded the hot dishes onto the cart, hoping somebody would show up before he got done loading. He'd ask them to walk at the front of the cart since he could barely see over the top of it. He smiled a sneaky smile. The haints would get them first and give him time to make a getaway.

He slowly took the last of the dishes out one by one, straining his ears in hope of hearing the footsteps of a nurse or a nun coming down the hall. The only sound was the slurp of the water draining out of the machine.

He'd have to push the cart all by himself. He wheeled it out the door and switched off the light. That made it even darker, but he knew if he made it down the tunnel once, he sure wasn't going to come back again to snap off the light. One overhead light bulb, where the tunnel turned right, glowed dimly.

The tunnel stretched far ahead into the darkness. Looked like a mile. Oliver wanted to run and push that cart ninety miles an hour, but he knew dishes would fly every which way if he did that. Maybe he could just speed up a little. The dishes clattered some, but they didn't fall off, so he kept going, looking straight ahead. He didn't dare look to the side or behind for fear the shimmery, green ghost that he saw in Mississippi would bust out and snatch him.

He pictured the dead body that nobody rang the bell for last week. "Mr. Spirit," he thought, "I hope you went with the body and ain't stuck in this tunnel looking for him."

Oliver maneuvered the cart on to the right turn. Now he could see moonlight coming through the window of the back door. The special diets kitchen was the last room on the right. He opened the door, pushed the cart in, carefully pulled the door toward him until he heard it click, then hit the back door running. Boogedy, boogedy! Across the street and into his house.

Whew!

Grandma was sleeping on the couch with her leg propped up on a pillow. Oliver noticed the blue and white star quilt pulled up around her shoulders. Grandma loved that quilt so much. Her mama had made it, and she'd brought it all the way here from Mississippi. Oliver tiptoed over and kissed her on the forehead. She opened her eyes a little and smiled at him. "Thanks, Baby. You were a big help tonight. I believe my leg is doing better already."

Oliver imagined himself repeating the long, dark walk that he just lived through. He might not be as lucky the second time.

"Glad your leg is better, Grandma," Oliver said, nodding his head, "And I hope it stay that way FOREVER!"

Beginnings
Tuberculosis Treatment in Colorado Springs

Oliver's scary walk down the tunnel at St. Francis Hospital is based on fact. He was right when he thought dead bodies were wheeled down the tunnel.

The original St. Francis Hospital was one of many tuberculosis treatment centers that began in 1890 and continued through the 1940s. The nurses knew the disease was spread by germs, so they wheeled the bodies of the tuberculosis patients from the hospital through a tunnel under Pikes Peak Avenue. It went directly to a crematorium located near the Deaf and Blind School, where the bodies were cremated. You can still see the tall white chimney of the crematorium on the north side of Pikes Peak Avenue across from the St. Francis building.

Taking bodies down a tunnel rather than outside was just one of many ways that people were careful after 1900 when tuberculosis began to cause death all over the country.

Here are some other changes that happened at that time: women used to wear dresses that went past their ankles, and dress lengths became shorter so they wouldn't pick up germs from the ground; most men in the early 1900s wore beards, but a clean-shaven face became popular when men didn't want germs living in their beards; ice cream cones were invented to take the place of reusable glass containers, called penny-licks, that didn't get washed between customers; disposable Dixie cups replaced tin dippers that people shared; Kleenex became a popular substitute for cloth handkerchiefs; more playgrounds were built to give children plenty of fresh air and sunshine.

What exactly is this disease that changed so many everyday habits? Tuberculosis has been around since civilization began and is found in all parts of the world. It is an infection of the lungs that causes chest pain, shortness of breath, and coughing so severe that patients cough up blood. It was also called consumption because people became very thin like the disease was "consuming" them. As their lungs continued to fail, victims became weaker and weaker and then died.

From the 1880s until World War II, TB was the biggest health threat in the United States. It attacked young and old alike and caused twenty percent of all American deaths during that time.

The scariest part? There was no vaccine or medicine for it. No one knew exactly how it spread or how long the germs lasted. But doctors did agree that fresh air and sunshine led some people to recover from this deadly disease. They recommended that people go to the western mountain states where the climate might save their lives.

That is why Henry Sachs, who we learned about in Chapter One, came to Colorado Springs. Many other people came, too. At one time, one-third of the population of Colorado Springs had tuberculosis.

To prepare for all these sick people coming into town, a new type of health center, called a sanitorium, was built. There were ten large sanitorium centers in Colorado Springs plus other smaller centers. Many local residents added sleeping porches to their homes and rented these rooms to tuberculosis patients.

Charles Fox Gardiner was a frontier doctor who lived at that time. He worked in western mountain towns and knew the Ute Indians who lived near his home in Meeker, Colorado. The Ute tepees, with fresh air circulation, gave Dr. Gardiner an idea. He invented an eight-sided hut, called a "sanitary tent," that would give tuberculosis patients more fresh air and sunshine than a hospital room. These huts had the same furnishings as a hospital room, but housed only one person each to prevent the spread of germs.

The large treatment centers soon had rows and rows of huts. The Woodmen Center had 205.

In 1921, the discovery of the bacteria that caused tuberculosis allowed a vaccine to be developed. During World War II, antibiotics were developed to treat the disease. At last, the deadly plague was coming to an end.

But before the sanitoriums closed completely, one of Oliver's first jobs after high school was as an orderly at the Cragmor Sanitorium. He had personal contact with sick patients—bringing them meals and emptying their bedpans if they were too weak to use the bathroom. This close exposure to the germs made him test positive for tuberculosis for the rest of his life even though he never developed the disease.

Wouldn't it be fun to see a real TB hut from those early days of Colorado Springs? You can do it and even look inside the room! There are several around town. You might be surprised at how large they are. If you count the sides, you will see they have eight, just like Dr. Gardiner designed them. The furnishings are exactly like those the patients would have used.

You can visit a tuberculosis hut at any of these locations:

1. The Pioneers Museum, 215 South Tejon Street. It is inside the building, on the third floor, as part of a large, interesting exhibit named "City of Sunshine," that will tell you much more about tuberculosis treatment in Colorado Springs.

2. Margery Reed Memorial Park by Cascade and Jackson Streets. This hut is outside.

3. A hut from the large Woodmen Sanatorium, now Mount St. Francis, is also located outside at 7665 Assisi Heights.

The real Grandma (Lucreasie Williams) in front of St. Francis Chapel.

Photo courtesy of Lucy Bell

Tuberculosis treatment outdoor huts at the Woodmen Sanitorium.

Photo courtesy of Pikes Peak Library District Special Collections

CHAPTER 3

THE SECRET HIDEOUT

Colorado Springs, Colorado
July, 1943

Two loaves for a nickel! That's what the Town House Bakery charged for day-old bread. One Saturday morning, Grandma found an extra nickel in her apron pocket and sent Oliver down to get bread for the weekend. Oliver always stopped by the neighbor ladies to see if he should pick up some for them. Miz Bass said no, but Miz Duncan gave him a nickel.

Miz Bailey, behind the counter at the bakery, put the loaves in paper bags.

"Thank you, young man," she said smiling at Oliver when he gave her the two nickels.

One time Miz Bailey stopped by to visit Grandma, and Oliver remembered how she smelled just like fresh-baked bread, even when she wasn't in the bakery.

Oliver stopped at Miz Duncan's house, left her bread on the kitchen table, and closed the door behind him.

When he looked down the street, he couldn't believe his eyes! A big golden brown horse with a silvery white mane and tail was coming right

towards him. It looked like Trigger! Oliver wondered, could it be Roy
Rogers riding on it? But as they got close, he saw it wasn't Roy—just a
plain old white man. Not even wearing a cowboy hat. Oliver smiled up at
them anyway and gave a little wave.

The man didn't seem to see him, but the horse gave him a friendly
look. He watched until they were out of sight and all that was left was the
sunshine reflecting off that horse's swishing tail.

Oliver thought about sitting up in the balcony of the cool, dark Chief
Theater watching Roy Rogers and Trigger come to the rescue when mean
guys was doing something bad.

It seemed funny. Colored folks had to sit in the balcony, like they wasn't good seats or something. Oliver thought they were the best seats in the house. So did his friend, Hansy Heckle, but he had to sit down below with the rest of the white people.

Oliver gave Grandma the bread, and when he went out on the porch, he saw Sammy Brown coming—boogedy, boogedy.

"Hey, Sammy Yammy. What's your hurry, Yamhead?"

"Hey Popeye! Guess what! They building a secret hideout over in the field. Gonna be underground so nobody can see it."

Oliver stood up. "Oh, yeah? Who's doing it?"

"Jack and Cecil. Miz Stark almost catch 'em stealing her crab apples last night. They need a hideout so they can make a quick getaway."

Oliver smiled. Everybody called Miz Stark a witch because she grew cherries so big and black they jes' had to be poison. Even still, Oliver had swiped a few of her crab apples himself, and a hideout sounded like a good idea.

"Let's go take a look at it. Race you to the field!"

They got there fast and saw Cecil leaning on a big, iron shovel, and his younger brother, Jack, on his knees digging.

"Need any help?" Oliver called out.

"Sure do," Cecil answered. He had already marked off a rectangular area and scooped off the top layer of dirt. "We need somebody to haul the dirt away. Not gonna leave no sign that this hideout is here. It'll be top secret."

"Here comes Joe with the wagon now. You guys start loading up the dirt. Take it away and spread it out so there's no suspicious looking piles any place. Okay?"

Pretty soon the Twins, Billy and Bobby, showed up to help with the digging. Oliver never could tell them apart. The girls in the neighborhood said they was so good looking and claimed to know one from the other.

Oliver was glad to see his friend Hansy coming, too. He could help with the hauling. Hansy was Courtney's little brother. Their family had moved into the neighborhood from Germany. Oliver teased him that he looked like one of the Katzenjammer Kids in the comics.

Everybody worked all afternoon. After supper, the usual neighborhood kids came to play tincan nerky. Those that hadn't heard about the hideout yet wanted to dig instead of play. That was all right with Cecil, Jack, Joe, and the Twins. They'd had enough digging for one day.

It took almost two weeks, but finally, the hole was big enough for four or five kids to sit in at the same time.

Oliver went to the hideout early Saturday morning. Cecil was still giving orders. "Now we need a roof. Everybody go look for something that'll fit 'cross the top of this hideout."

People in the neighborhood were always throwing out junk and trash. Oliver and Sammy went looking around. They found a few stray boards and boxes and were headed back to the field when they saw Joe tearing up from Shooks Run all excited.

When Joe first moved to the neighborhood from Texas, seemed like he was always braggin' about how great things was there, like they didn't know nothing in Colorado Springs. It made Oliver mad, yet and still, Joe always did seem to be full of good ideas.

"Everybody meet at the hideout," Joe yelled. "I found somethin' great!" Just like Joe, Oliver thought, talkin' 'bout his smart, Texas ways.

Joe leaped into the hole. Cecil and Jack followed him. Oliver and Sammy got in next. Hansy and the Twins came running across the field. There wasn't enough room for them to fit in the hideout, so they sprawled out on their stomachs, leaning over the edge to hear what Joe had to say.

"I found jes' what we need. Somebody threw away an old mattress spring down at Shooks Run. I dragged it part way up the bank, but I need help gettin' it over here. I think it'll fit good. We'll have to put it crosswise, and there'll be spaces on both sides, but that's O.K. cause that's how we can get in."

"Let's go get it now!" Jack said. "I'll help you."

"Me, too!" everybody hollered.

"Wait a minute," Billy said. "Won't we have to carry it past Grandpa Duncan's house? You know he always out on the porch watching everything goin' on."

"You right," agreed Cecil. "He'd never let us go by without asking what we be doing with a bedspring."

Joe was quiet, thinking it over. Oliver figured he'd come up with something.

"We gonna have to do it tonight. Who can meet me at Shooks Run after it get dark?"

Oliver knew he'd catch a whipping if Grandma saw him sneaking out of the house that late, so he didn't say anything.

Everybody looked at Cecil, but he said, "Cain't do it tonight."

Then Bobby spoke up. "Our uncle is visitin' us, and he's sleepin' in our bed. Me and Billy's sleeping downstairs on the couch." He looked at his brother with a sly grin, and they answered together, "We'll be there!"

The next day Oliver could hardly wait for Sunday School to be over. When he got to the field, he couldn't see the hideout at all. The boys had put twigs and dirt and weeds into the bedspring till it blended right in.

Sammy ran up to him. "We gonna have some fun in this hideout! When we swipe crab apples, old Miz Stark won't never catch us."

"Nosirree," Oliver said. "We gonna make a clean getaway."

The next day Oliver got most of his chores done and decided he'd walk down to the hideout. Jack and Cecil were just crawling out. "Hey, Popeye. How ya doin'?" Jack greeted.

"We got us some apples," Cecil said, pulling one out of the front of his shirt. "Want one?"

"Thanks!" Oliver bit into the firm, red skin and licked the juice from his lips.

"We're on our way to the movies. It's Roy Rogers. Think you can come?" Oliver shrugged his shoulders. "Cain't. Got no money. I just came by to look at the hideout."

"Okay, see you tonight for tin-can nerky," Cecil said, as they headed downtown.

Oliver slid down under the bedspring roof and leaned against the wall. The damp dirt felt good against his back. He wished he did have some money to go see Roy Rogers and Trigger. He thought about the friendly horse he'd seen a few days ago. Wonder what it would be like to ride a horse. You'd be sittin' up high, bouncin' up and down. Sure would be fun!

Oliver stopped daydreaming, slid out of the clubhouse, and started home.

Grandma was sitting in the rocker on the front porch. Her thin legs ending in her favorite button-top boots stretched out in front of her. A wisp of gray hair escaped her head-rag.

As Oliver got closer he could smell something good coming from the kitchen.

"What that I smell, Grandma?"

"You smell somethin' from way out there?" Grandma laughed. "What you think it smell like?"

"Smell like sweet potato pie," Oliver guessed, rubbing his stomach.

"You right. Go get yo'self a piece. But after that I need somebody to pull weeds out the garden. You hear?" Grandma called, as Oliver scampered past her and into the kitchen.

"Yes, Grandma," Oliver called back as he eased the warm piece of pie onto a plate and then attacked it with his fork.

Oliver savored the last bite and then went out the back door to the garden. The rhubarb's big, flat leaves spread out on the ground, and the stem part that Grandma made into pie was streaked with red. The corn came up to Oliver's chest. Some people called dandelions weeds, but Oliver knew better—Grandma made wine out of them. She made medicine out of Jimson weed, but that was growing over in the ditch, not in the garden.

Oliver picked weeds around everything except the plant with yellow flowers that was taller than he was. He'd pull it out if he could. It was nasty! Every fall Grandma would dig up the roots and put them in a jar to soak over winter to make asifidity water. Grandma made them drink it. She called it spring tonic and said it would help their digestion and make them strong. Oliver thought the only strong thing about it was the smell. By springtime, the root had turned to a mess of black gunk in the bottom of the jar.

Oliver's cousins in Mississippi told him their grandma put the root in a bag and made them wear it around their necks when they went to school. Oliver couldn't decide which was worse. It would be embarrassing to smell so bad around your friends. Yet you could take the bag off when your grandma wasn't looking. But there was no getting away from drinking outta that jar when Grandma was standing there waiting for you to swallow.

Oliver's thoughts were interrupted by Grandma's alarmed voice. "Lawd, have mercy!"

He threw the weeds down and ran to the front of the house where Miz Brown stood, shifting back and forth on her feet, looking all jumpy.

"What's wrong?" he asked.

Miz Brown answered. "They's been a bad accident. A big, yeller horse fell in a deep hole out in the middle of the field. It's turrible. They say the horse done broke its leg. Man riding it got throwed off. Guess he's not hurt too bad—just banged up."

"Mercy, mercy," Grandma was shaking her head. "They gonna have to shoot that horse. Horse can't live with a broke leg."

Oliver had clapped his hand over his mouth when Miz Brown started the story. Then tears started running down his cheeks at Grandma's words.

"What's wrong wit' you, Boy?" Grandma looked at him suspiciously. "You know something 'bout all this?"

"I – I- think I saw the horse, Grandma, a few days ago. Looked just like Trigger."

"You young-uns play out in that field every night. You ever see a big hole out there?"

Oliver looked down at his shoes.

"Answer up, Boy," Grandma commanded, scowling.

Miz Brown was looking at Oliver, waiting for an answer, too.

"Yes, ma'am," Oliver answered slowly. "Guess there was a hole out there, all right."

"A hole big enough for a horse to fall in?"

Oliver didn't answer. He glanced up at Miz Brown and saw her staring down the street.

"My, my, y'all, look!" she exclaimed, "A PO-lice car. I do believe it's coming here."

"Sho nuff," Grandma said. She began to nervously finger the collection of safety pins she kept on the front of her dress, as the policeman pulled to a stop in front of the house and stuck his head out the window.

Oliver's heart began to pound.

The officer motioned to Oliver with a lift of his chin, "This your boy?" he asked Miz Brown.

"No, sir. My boy's at home."

"This here's my grandson," Grandma answered.

"Well, he needs to be down at the field at 6 o'clock this evening. Your boy, too, Ma'am. Every young man in the neighborhood needs to be there. They've got some work to do tonight. They've got a big hole to fill up."

The police officer looked at Oliver, "You know what I'm talking about, young man?"

Oliver didn't say anything. He'd stopped crying but the tears left dusty tracks down his cheeks. His lower lip quivered, but he saw Grandma giving him the answer-up look.

He sniffed and nodded. "Yes, sir."

The policeman, satisfied, drove away.

"You-uns dug that hole. I don't believe it. Sure enough can find some new kind of devilment to get into, every minute. Mm.mm.mm." Grandma said shaking her head.

"Did Sammy dig, too?" Miz Brown didn't wait for Oliver's answer. She was halfway down the block to ask Sammy herself.

Oliver went in the back room and threw himself across the old, raggedy couch. He didn't care if Grandma was going to make him go get a crab apple switch so she could whup him. He didn't care if he had to work till midnight carrying dirt to fill up the hole. The onliest thing he cared about in the whole world was that a beautiful, friendly horse had to die. He let the tears come out and cried and cried as if his heart was breaking. Because it was.

Beginnings
Segregation in Colorado Springs

When Oliver talked about black and white people having to sit in different sections of the movie theater, he was talking about segregation.

If you were an African American child living at that time, what would that mean to you?

If you lived in the South, you would go to an all-black school. Often the black schools did not have enough money, so your books would be old and used and probably out of date.

If you rode on a city bus, you would have to sit in the farthest back seats. If you went shopping downtown and got thirsty, you would drink at the drinking fountain marked "Colored," not the one marked "White." The bathrooms were separate, too. If you planned to catch a train to go visit a relative, you would sit in the Colored waiting room until the train arrived.

General Palmer, who founded Colorado Springs, didn't believe in segregation, so he did not allow separate schools. Oliver's friends, the Heckle family, came from Germany, and they all went to Helen Hunt School with other white, black, and Hispanic children who lived in the neighborhood.

But General Palmer couldn't control private businesses. Most of the restaurants in town had white owners. If you were a black child, you would have to go around to the back of the restaurant to get your food, and you couldn't eat it inside the building. The only day you could swim at the public swimming pool was Wednesday because that was the weekly cleaning day, which they did after you left.

It wasn't fair, and in the 1960s, Martin Luther King, Jr. inspired people in the South to protest unfair treatment. One type of protest was the sit-in where black people went to restaurants that would only serve white people and sat at the counter anyway.

In Colorado Springs, the protests began in 1945. Local resident, Joe Morgan, who was ninety-two in 2018, recalls going into the Walgreen's

Drugstore at 12 South Tejon with his brother where they were refused service.

The next day they and two other friends, all students at Colorado Springs High School, returned to the store, sat at the counter, and ordered milkshakes. Back in the kitchen, the cook poured salt into the milkshakes and stirred it in. The waitress set the order down in front of the boys along with their bill. It tasted so bad that they could not swallow one sip. When the group refused to pay for the shakes, the owner called the police. In just a few minutes, a burly, white policeman arrived. He tasted the milkshakes and said he wouldn't pay for them either, and the boys were free to go.

Protests continued. Finally, a 1947 suit filed in District Court against Walgreen's came to trial in July of 1950. The trial lasted five days. On the afternoon of July 19th, the jury of four women and two men deliberated only an hour and a half before returning a verdict in favor of Walgreen's refusal to serve black customers. A motion for a new trial was denied, but the fight was not over.

Charles Banks, leader of the local National Association for the Advancement of Colored People (NAACP), led a second sit-in at Walgreen's that overturned the first outcome. Charles Banks had been fighting for equal rights for black citizens since the 1920s. At that time, the Ku Klux Klan (KKK) was very active in Colorado. Clarence Morley, elected governor in 1924, and Denver mayor, Benjamin Stapleton, were both members of the KKK. The courts, legislature, and police force were dominated by Klan members.

When Kimbal Stroud, oldest sister of Effie (whom you read about in Chapter Two), purchased a house on Mesa Drive, the local KKK burned it down the next night.

They decided Charles Banks would be next. One night his little daughter, Charlotte, woke up to see the house next door on fire, and men in white robes running around with torches. They looked like ghosts to her. "Daddy, Daddy!" she screamed, "The ghosts are burning down the yellow house!" The KKK had meant to burn down Charles' home, but they got the wrong house.

Charles continued to work for change in the legislature for the next twenty years. He based his stand on the Constitution of the State of Colorado that had an unenforced law on the books from the 1880s prohibiting racial discrimination in public places.

Segregated public facilities finally came to an end in 1957 after the Colorado Civil Rights Division began investigating complaints and ruled that people could not be treated differently because of the color of their skin.

The home that little Charlotte lived in when she was frightened by seeing ghosts with torches is at 314 West Williamette Avenue. It was originally owned by Dr. Isaac Edward Moore, the first black physician in Colorado Springs, and was used as a hospital in the 1920s before it became a private residence rented by the Banks family. The yellow house next door mistakenly burned down by the KKK was never replaced. The vacant lot was purchased by the Morgan Memorial Chapel at 701 North Spruce Street and is currently used as a church parking lot.

The balcony of the Chief Theater in the 1940s

Photo courtesy of Pikes Peak Library District Special Collections

Negroes to Use Monument Pool Each Wednesday

The swimming pool in Monument valley park will be reserved for use of colored people each Wednesday, as an experiment undertaken by the park department, it was announced Saturday.

Life guards and swimming instructors will be on duty as on other days, the selection of Wednesday having been made by the park commission in response to requests from various negro organizations and individuals for the right to use the pool one day a week.

The park commission announced that the plan was a trial to determine whether patronage will warrant continuation of the schedule on this basis.

Latest letter to the commission on the matter came from Tandy Stroud, 741 N. Spruce St., well known negro leader.

Colo Spgs Sunday Gazette & Telegraph 7/21/1940 4:6

Negroes to use Monument pool each Wednesday. (1940, July 21). *Colo Spgs Sunday Gazette & Telegraph.* [Microfilm]. (Reel 4, Microfilm 6).

CHAPTER 4

ROCK OF AGES

Colorado Springs, Colorado
August, 1944

"Do I gotta wear the necktie, Grandma?" Oliver stood in the doorway of the kitchen, frowning at the dark blue tie hanging lopsided from the collar of his white dress shirt.

"Course you do. You goin' to Sunday school, ain't you? Come here, I'll tie it for you."

Oliver sighed and let Grandma work on the tie. The smell of Sunday biscuits filled the kitchen, and Oliver thought he probably could eat a couple more, but now that he was dressed for church, he knew Grandma wouldn't allow it. She wasn't about to let him go off with butter stains down his front.

Grandma sat down at the wooden table to enjoy another cup of coffee and gave him a smile of approval. It was a long walk to People's Methodist on St. Vrain Street. Grandma didn't feel up to going, and she was grateful that her grandson would be there in her place.

Oliver always gave Grandma a report about the Bible stories and songs he'd learned that day, but two things about Sunday school he'd never tell Grandma.

The first thing Grandma didn't know about was that People's Methodist, almost a mile north of their house on Colorado, was North-ender territory. He was the lone South-ender, and every Sunday ended the same. The minute they said the last amen and went out the door, the North-enders ganged up on him, and Oliver had to make a run for it.

The second secret that he didn't tell Grandma was that sometimes he'd walk down Colorado Avenue and instead of turning north on El Paso Street, he'd keep going west up to the railroad tracks and catch a ride to church on the slow moving freight train that went north. He'd grab the handrail and ride on the outside open door of the boxcar. When it slowed down for the curve at St. Vrain, he'd jump off and be right at People's Church.

He had to climb Hobo Hill on his way to catch the freight train. One time, a hobo resting against a tree called to him, "Hey Boy, you got a dime you could lend me?" Oliver put his head down and kept walking. All he had was a nickel for the offering plate. If he did have a dime, he wouldn't give it to the hobo.

Hobos often knocked on Grandma's door asking for a handout. She'd usually give them a sandwich, but she started wondering why more hobos were knocking on her door than anybody else's. Come to find out, the hobos marked an X on the back of the fence to tell their friends, "Good people live here."

Oliver remembered Grandma scowling and muttering to herself, "We may be good people, but we ain't no café." Yet and still, she always found something for them.

No trains were going by the church when Sunday school let out. Oliver had to have a good sneaky plan to get away from the North-enders and run back home. Last Sunday's escape route worked great. He'd skuddled out the side door of the church, cut down the alley running fast as he could, and turned into Tony's back yard and up the steps to Tony's grocery store on Monument Street.

He remembered Tony looked up from behind the counter. "Hey Oliver, what you puffin' about? Your shirt tail don't look so good hangin' out like that."

"Oh, nuthin," he'd answered, tucking in his shirt and peering out the front window straining to catch sight of Bud, his brother Cy, and Donald. Junior and his brothers were visiting some relatives in St. Louis and weren't in Sunday school that morning, so he didn't have to worry about them.

Coast is clear, Oliver thought, sliding out the front door. "Bye, Tony!" he called over his shoulder, then ran from Monument to El Paso Street and past the railroad tracks, making it home free.

Yeah, that plan worked good, but he couldn't use it two weeks in a row. The North-enders weren't no dummies. They'd probably make it to Tony's store before he did.

This time he had a different plan, and he couldn't wait to try it. He headed for the door, but Grandma stopped him.

"Finish your milk," she ordered. "And slow down. Don't spill it."

Oliver carefully drank the milk.

"Leavin' kind of early, ain't you?" Grandma gave him her suspicious stare.

Oliver shrugged.

"Come straight home after Sunday school's over. Hear?"

Oliver nodded, closed the screen door behind him, and headed down the street.

He grinned to himself as he remembered the great plan that came to him right before he went to sleep last night.

The North-enders always had time to gather up rocks to throw at him, and he never had time to pick up any to throw back, so this time he'd be ready. Oliver gathered rocks and arranged four piles, spacing them from the railroad tracks to the street.

He knew he could outrun all of the North-enders except for Donald, who had longer legs than anybody, but today Oliver had part two of his plan to take care of Donald.

He was early, so he just walked on down El Paso Street until he caught sight of the tall, pointy steeple. On the top of the steeple, an iron rod rose up out of a small metal ball and pointed even farther into the sky.

The outside walls had a design of half circles in rows. Oliver thought they looked like bunches of little suns coming up.

The grownups went in the two tall doors at the front, but the Sunday school kids went in the side door and down to the basement. The windows of the church opened to the summer air, and when Oliver got close, he could hear the people singing:

> *Oh, I woke up dis mornin' wid mah min'*
> *An' it was stayed,*
> *Stayed on Jesus*
> *Hal-le-lu,*

> *Hal-le-lu,*
> *Hal-le-lu yah!*

Oliver slowed down so he could hear his favorite verse, and he hummed along with it.

> *De devil can't catch you in your min'*
> *If you keep it*
> *Stayed on Jesus.*

Oliver was still humming when he walked up the three outside cement steps and then down again on another set of steps that took him to the basement.

A picture of Jesus welcoming little children hung on one wall, and an old, out-of-tune piano with yellow keys stood across from it.

The boys and girls had separate classrooms. Oliver stopped at the door of his classroom and scanned the room to see who he was up against.

Junior was back and looked like he had on a new suit. He turned around to stare at Oliver and then nudged Bud, who nudged Donald, who was leaning back on his chair with his big, old, long legs stretched out in front of him. Oliver smiled to himself when he thought how his secret plan would take care of Donald.

Oliver slid onto his chair, and everybody faced forward when Miz Douglas spoke. "Children, please bow your heads in prayer. *Heavenly Father, we ask your blessing on these children gathered here today. Help them to follow your word always. Guide their feet on the path of righteousness. We ask in Jesus' name. Amen.*"

Everyone raised their heads, and Miz Douglas continued, "Today we are going to hear the Bible story of the Lost Sheep and what Jesus taught the people about that. Have any of you ever lost something that was so important to you that you went back to look for it?"

"I lost my milk money, and when I went back to get it, somebody had stole it," Cy told her.

"Somebody stole my basketball!" Junior said, glaring at Bud.

"Did not!" Bud mouthed back.

Miz Douglas put her finger to her lips, and all the talking stopped. She paused until everybody's eyes were focused on her, and then she continued in her clear, calm voice. "We are not talking about stealing today. That might be a good lesson for another day. Today we are going to hear the story that Jesus told about a shepherd who lost one of his sheep."

Oliver listened closely to the story so he could tell it to Grandma when he got home. He pictured ninety-nine fuzzy animals all crowding together and bumping into each other. That's a lotta sheep, he thought. How would anybody ever count 'em? They look alike, and they never be standing still. Shepherds had dogs to help, but dogs cain't count. Oliver caught himself getting off track. He better tune back in to Miz Douglas, who was finishing up:

"So children, remember this: You are God's little lambs, and He loves every one of you just as much as that shepherd loved his sheep. Amen?"

"Amen!" everybody answered back.

Miz Douglas held up the offering plate and looked around, "Junior, don't you look fine this morning! We missed you last Sunday. I hope you had a beautiful time with your family in St. Louis. Would you like to pass the offering plate for us?"

"Yes, Ma'am," Junior answered, with a proud little grin about how good he looked.

Oliver dug in his pocket for his nickel and plunked it down on the green velvet lining of the gold plate.

Miss Douglas placed the collection plate on top of the piano, sat down, played a few chords, then nodded to the boys to stand up, and they all sang "Jesus Loves Me."

It was time for the final prayer. Miss Douglas began:

Lord, we thank you for this beautiful morning. Oliver scooted forward on the gray folding chair. *Go with us as we leave this holy place.* Oliver's toes touched the floor. *Guide us on your path until we meet here again.* Oliver leaned forward and lowered his heels. *Amen.* BAM! His feet hit the floor, and he was up the steps and out the door.

He took off running and didn't look back. When he got close to the railroad tracks, he was pretty sure he'd outrun everybody except Donald. Good. Time to put part two of his plan into action.

He stopped short at his first pile of rocks and stuck his leg out across the path. In his imagination, it was perfect. Donald would be coming so fast he wouldn't see Oliver's leg, and he'd fall flat on his face, giving Oliver time to load up with rocks and scare him off.

Oliver waited and waited with his leg stuck out. His standing leg was getting tired. Finally, he looked behind him and saw Donald chugging up the path. He was way too far behind for the tripping-over-the leg-plan to work. Nobody else was coming, so he didn't need his rock piles.

Shucks. So much for great plans you get in the night. Oliver pulled his leg back and looked around on the ground for a stick. He found a good one and balanced it it on his shoulder. Donald was close enough to see him do it. He stopped, took his glasses off, shoved them into his pocket, and picked up a stick. When he was face to face with Oliver, Donald put his stick on his shoulder.

They circled around each other. Knocking the stick off was the same as delivering the first blow. If you knocked the stick off you better be ready to defend yourself from a punch.

Round and round they circled—slow enough not to get dizzy or lose the sticks.

"Where's all your buddies?" Oliver taunted.

"Don't need 'em," Donald answered.

Sometimes the sticks would wobble a little, but the boys kept walking in a slow circle. It was starting to get boring.

Finally, they stopped circling and stood looking at each other. Oliver knew he wasn't about to knock Donald's stick off. He wanted to get in the first punch.

They stood and stood some more.

"Oh man, I'm going home!" Donald said, swinging around away from Oliver and catching his stick when it fell. He didn't look back.

Oliver threw his stick down and headed home, too, passing the rest of his rock piles. When he got to the last one, he tucked his shirt in and straightened his tie.

He saw Grandma sitting on the porch in her rocking chair listening to her church program on the radio. Oliver could hear the Mills Brothers singing "Rock of Ages" in the background. Grandma kept rocking to the slow rhythm of the old hymn, and her up-and- down glance and slight nod let Oliver know he'd passed inspection, and he wasn't late.

"Hi, Grandma," he smiled. "I got a good Jesus story to tell you today. You ever hear tell 'bout a sheep what got lost?"

Beginnings
People's Methodist Episcopal Church

Oliver always remembered his adventures with the North-ender boys. Eventually, they all became friends. They went to the same high school, and some of them worked together at the Green Parrot Shining Parlor. Oliver and Donald were still friends when they were adults.

Oliver never forgot the church, either. As a boy, he liked the pointy steeple with the metal rod and ball, and the decorations that reminded him of little suns coming up. The official name of this decoration is "half-cove fancy wood shingles." It is a perfect example of Queen Anne Style architecture, which was popular in England before Colorado was even a state.

How in the world did such a building style get to a black community in Colorado Springs?

To answer this question, we have to look at how People's Methodist Church got started. When churches first begin, they usually don't have a building at all. They begin with a group of people who have the same ideas about religion. Usually one person gets the idea going.

The person responsible in our story was a man named Frank Loper. He was born a slave on a cotton plantation in Mississippi in 1850. His owner was Jefferson Davis, the President of the Confederate states during the Civil War. At the end of the Civil War, in 1865, Frank and his parents were free, but they stayed to work at the plantation.

In 1878, Frank, now a young man, began working for Jefferson Davis' daughter, Margaret Hayes. When she moved to Colorado Springs in 1886, Frank came with her as an employee at her mansion on Cascade Avenue.

He and other former slave families met for prayer downtown, near the Antlers Hotel, where they began to plan for a church of their own. Their dream became reality in 1904 with the completion of People's Methodist Episcopal Church on the corner of East St. Vrain and Royer.

The builder and contractor was a Methodist minister named Reverend C.S. Steinmetz. He liked the Queen Anne Style architecture. The year before, in 1903, he had built his own church, Calvary Methodist, on the corner of Wahsatch and Boulder Streets, in this style. He was ready to do another one.

People began raising money for the project. The first thing they needed was a foundation for the building, and they wanted it to have a basement. Garfield Green ran a hauling business, delivering ice and hauling away ashes with his horse and wagon. He was the only man in town who had both a horse and a scoop, and he signed on to dig the basement where Oliver would later go to Sunday school. William Dunlap, a stonemason, built the foundation. The congregation continued to grow, and the original building at St. Vrain and Royer Streets has been in constant use since 1904.

Remember the old, out-of-tune piano in Oliver's Sunday School room? It had good reason to be out of tune.

In 1935, Colorado Springs experienced a historic flood. Homes and buildings all over town were flooded like never before. Ten years before Oliver, a man named Richard Walker attended Sunday school in that same room, and he would never forget the high water that surged down the streets of his neighborhood.

He remembers going over to the church after the floodwaters had gone down, and when he peeked into the basement window, he had a big surprise. The basement was still flooded. Bobbing along on top of the water was the big, heavy piano! Richard ran home to tell his mom, "I didn't know pianos could float!"

The men pumped the water out of the basement. The piano was too heavy to move, so they left it there to dry out. A few months later, it played just as well as it had before and was used for many more years.

Are you sorry that you can't see the real building that has such a fascinating past? Don't be sorry. The Department of the Interior recently placed this building on the National Register of Historic Places. It is just a few blocks from downtown Colorado Springs at 527 East St.Vrain and is presently the home of the Independent Missionary Baptist Church. Down in the basement you can see the Sunday school rooms, and when the door to one of the storage rooms is opened, you can see a section of the foundation that William Dunlap built in 1904.

Do you wish you could meet some of the people involved in this story? You can! Franklin Macon was raised by the former slave, Frank Loper, after he married Franklin's aunt in 1931. Frank became a Tuskegee airman during World War II.

Richard Walker, the boy who saw the piano floating, is still a member of People's Methodist church. His father, Dr. William Walker, was one of the first black physicians in Colorado Springs. Richard served in World War II as a nineteen-year-old support sergeant based in Weymouth, England in 1944, at the time of the Normandy invasion.

Both Franklin Macon and Richard Walker are in their nineties and live in Colorado Springs. They are in good health and enjoy sharing their memorable stories.

People's Methodist was the third black church founded in Colorado Springs. The first was Payne Chapel in 1875, built on land donated by General Palmer. The second was St. John's Baptist in 1897. Trinity Missionary Baptist Church began in 1913; The Church of God in Christ, now known as the Morgan Memorial Chapel, began in 1919; and Friendship Baptist started in 1947. All of these churches are active today and would be glad to give you more information on their exciting history.

People's Methodist Church at 527 East St. Vrain Street today. This is
the original 1904 building that is on the National Register of Historic
Places.

Photo courtesy of Lucy Bell

The real Donald (in the middle) with his two younger brothers in front
of People's Methodist Church (circa 1945).

Photo courtesy of Dorothy Patterson

CHAPTER 5

YOKUM IN THE DARK

Colorado Springs, Colorado
June, 1945

Oliver stopped to admire the green parrot with stretched-out wings and long tail feathers painted on the window below the words "Green Parrot Shining Parlor." He felt lucky to get this great summer job as a shoeshine boy.

He went inside to check in with Dad Kirven. Dad was "poppin rags" on the shoes of an elderly customer sitting in one of the four inside chairs. Right hand. Left hand. Pop! Dad's rhythmic snapping of the polishing cloth made the customer smile.

Dad was kind and generous. He kept a barrel by the front door where people could discard old shoes. He put on new heels and soles, shined them up so they looked brand new, and gave them to needy families.

He was patient with the boys and never yelled at them. But, if they came late to work or didn't do a good job, he told them they didn't need to come back the next day.

Oliver knew all the other shoeshine boys: Sammy, his friend from school; Johnny and Bud from his Sunday School class at People's

Methodist; and John and Justus, whose dad had started a church on the West Side way back in 1919. Everybody in the neighborhood knew the Twins, Billy and Bobby, who were fourteen and went to South Junior. They liked to instigate fights and act tough. Folks called them Double Trouble.

Dad motioned for Oliver to head outside where six chairs lined the storefront facing out to Pikes Peak Avenue.

A tall Camp Carson soldier stepped down from one of the chairs, his combat boots shining. He handed Bud a quarter and a ten-cent tip. Shining a soldier's boots was Oliver's favorite job.

Sammy was working on the black shoes of a businessman. Justus was assembling a bottle of white liquid polish and black paste that he'd need for a man with two-tone shoes. Oliver had never done that kind. Two-tone customers had to pay thirty-five cents instead of the regular twenty-five.

Oliver didn't have to wait long for his first customer. A woman soldier sat down on one of the chairs and beckoned Oliver to come over. The Army women were called WACS and wore brown oxfords as part of their uniform.

Oliver checked to make sure he had brown polish in his box and greeted the lady. "Good morning, Ma'am. Shine today?"

The lady smiled and nodded. "Do a good job, please, young man. I have inspection this afternoon."

Dad gave each boy a notebook to write down the hours that they worked. At the end of the week, they took the notebook to Mrs. Kirven who stamped the page and paid them. Oliver liked to show Grandma the stamped pages and total money earned. "My, my!" she'd say. "Ain't that somethin'!"

One July morning, the boys stood outside waiting for customers when a new guy named Willie showed up for work. He looked about thirteen and had conked hair slicked back against his head. "One O'Clock Jump" was playing on Dad's radio, and Willie did a fancy dance step to the music.

That caught Billy and Bobby's attention. They swaggered up to Willie with their shoulders thrown back.

"First day?" Bobby asked.

"First day here." Willie put one hand on his hip and raised his chin. "I shined shoes before."

Billy stepped closer. "You don't know how to dance."

Bobby closed in on the other side. "Sumpin's wrong witcha hair."

"Hey!" Dad Kirven called. "Bobby, come in here. Need you to put new heels on some shoes. People be pickin' 'em up in an hour. Billy, you help him."

The Twins followed Dad inside, and Willie joined Oliver on the sidewalk. "Those guys think they tough, or somethin'?"

"Listen here," Willie talked low into Oliver's ear. "They don't know tough. I only been in this town for two months. Ah'm from Shi-Cog-Go." Oliver had heard of Chicago before, but Willie made it sound dangerous.

"Know what I got?" He lifted his shirt so Oliver could see something stuck in his belt.

"Look like a knife."

"That's what it is, and Ah knows how to use it," Willie said with one nod of his head.

A rainy Saturday left all the Green Parrot chairs empty. The boys showed up anyway. An hour rolled by, but dark clouds still hid Pikes Peak.

Billy spoke up. "You ever been in Dad Kirven's basement?"

"Basement?" Sammy scratched his head. "Didn't know he had one."

"Well, he do. The whole thing below the ground. Dark as anything. We'll ask Dad Kirven if we can show you."

Justus and John had to go home to help get the church ready for tomorrow's Sunday service. Everybody else jumped up and followed the Twins. It sounded more interesting than sitting around in the rain.

"Go ahead," Dad Kirven told Billy. "Nothing down there except spiders. And my shoe-spray bench. You leave that alone, hear?"

Bobby turned on the light switch at the top of the stairs and stood by it. Billy led everybody else down the steep wooden steps to the damp floor enclosed by gray cement walls.

"See any spiders?" Sammy whispered.

"Just that one on your neck," Oliver joked.

Billy stood in the center of the basement. "Now here's how the game works."

"What game?" Johnny asked.

"The game we gonna teach you. Called Yokum in the Dark. Bobby's gonna turn off the light, and we all start moving. You cain't touch nobody. If anybody touches you, you have the right to hit him hard as you can. Turn off the lights, Bobby."

In a flash, it got darker than dark. Oliver stuck his hand in front of his face. He couldn't see it, even when he brought it so close it touched his nose. Everybody heard Bobby clambering down the steps. Then it was silent. Oliver couldn't decide if he should move or stay still. He thought about how hard the Twins could hit. He thought of something even scarier—the knife in Willie's belt.

Oliver could hear breathing and the sound of careful footsteps. I'll stay close to the wall, he thought. If I run into somebody, I better hit them first. He edged along the cold cement. His ears felt like they had doubled in size as he strained to catch every sound.

Oh, no! He'd reached the corner where the other wall began. He didn't want to turn around because he knew at least one person was behind him. But what if somebody was coming along the next wall in the opposite direction? The center of the room might be the safest place of all.

He moved away from the wall keeping his fingers against the cold cement, for balance, then let go and carefully stepped out toward the middle.

The cold, damp air smelled moldy. It made Oliver want to hold his nose, but he needed both arms ready for protection. He crept ten slow steps forward when he touched somebody. It's him or me, he thought. Cousin Frank's boxing lessons kicked in. He doubled up his right fist and swung with all his might. BAM! Crunch! The punch landed smack on somebody's nose! Whoever it was crumpled at his feet.

"YOW! Who did that? You broke my nose, you POSSUM BAIT! Turn those lights on NOW, Billy!"

Billy scrambled up the stairs for the light switch. Everybody else ran, changing places, not caring if they bumped into somebody or not. Oliver headed for a wall. He wanted to get out of the center for sure.

The big light bulb hanging from a cord in the ceiling came on bright and blinding.

The only one not running was Willie. He pulled himself up from the floor. Blood ran from his nose, into his mouth, and down his chin.

"All right, who did it? You gonna pay!" He patted the bulge at his waist.

Sammy pressed himself against the wall. "Not me!"

"Not me." Johnny had managed to get to the stairs and sat all straight like he was in Sunday school, his fingers clenching the bottom step.

"Not me," Bud answered under the light bulb's glare.

Oliver rubbed his right knuckles with his left hand where they still stung from the punch. "Not me," he lied in a weak voice. He was standing in the shadow of the shoe-spraying bench, and by the time he answered, Willie was glaring at the Twins.

"It's just a game," Billy sneered.

Bobby moved over next to Billy. "Cain't you take it?"

Willie looked like he wanted to take them both on, but he only had one free hand. He had to use the other one to keep wiping his nose with the bottom of his shirt. He stomped up the stairs, just missing Johnny's fingers. At the top, he flicked the light switch off and on.

"Dumb Sissy Game!" he snarled down at them and disappeared out the door.

The room was silent. Everybody, except the Twins, breathed a sigh of relief. Oliver was glad the Twins seemed to be taking credit for punching Willie in the nose. They probably each thought the other one did it.

Oliver broke the silence. "Maybe the rain stopped. Maybe they's customers."

"Rain ain't stopped and ain't no customers," Bobby declared folding his arms across his chest. "Time for Round Two of Yokum in the Dark."

"I'ma go see." Oliver scampered halfway up the steps before anybody could stop him.

"BABY!" Billy called after him.

Oliver didn't care. He opened the door fast, pulled the collar of his shirt up around his neck, and ran for home in the pouring rain and crashing thunder. The Twins could call him Baby for the next hunnert years. He could take that easier than another round of Yokum.

Beginnings
Job Opportunities Before and After General Palmer's Death

Oliver felt lucky to get his summer job at the Green Parrot Shining Parlor, and he was, because by the time he was born in 1933, many black jobs that General Palmer supported had disappeared.

After the Civil War, black people began moving to Colorado Springs because they'd heard about the fair treatment in General Palmer's town, and they wanted their children to have a better education than they would get in the South.

General Palmer welcomed new people. He paid his white and black workers the same wages for the same jobs. Black people could save money and start their own businesses.

Among the many businesses owned were livery stables, grocery stores, fuel and hauling services, tailoring and dressmaking shops, a dairy farm, two weekly newspapers, and a publishing company. Several blacks were self-employed in construction, catering, laundry services, landscaping, horse-breaking, and blacksmithing.

Constable Horace Shelby was an officer in the police department. Other blacks were employed as guards in the city jail. Charles Collins was the Riding Master at the popular Riding Academy. The entire staff of the Antlers Hotel from the headwaiter on down were black. Most of the hotels and the estates in the Old North End were maintained by black cooks, laundresses, maids, chauffeurs, butlers, gardeners, and nannies for the children.

Things were looking good for these people who were the children of slaves, and in some cases, had been slaves themselves.

But when Palmer died in 1909, things changed almost overnight. Many newcomers, with power in business and government, came from the South where they had benefited from segregation. They did not agree with Palmer's philosophy that black people should have the same jobs as whites.

If you were an African American child who moved to Colorado Springs after Palmer died, your mom or dad would probably have worked as a janitor or a maid or some other service occupation like hauling trash or shining shoes.

You'd have no chance of getting a job as a teacher. That would not happen until 1954. (Guess who it was! Remember Effie Stroud, who received the first Sachs scholarship to Colorado College? The first black teacher in Colorado Springs was Nina Stroud, Effie's little sister.)

But black people didn't give up. They "kept on keeping on" and "making a way where there was no way." The passage of the Civil Rights laws in the 1960s made a big difference in their opportunities.

What kind of work did Oliver have after his job of shining shoes? When he graduated from high school in 1951, he could only be hired for jobs considered "Negro work." After his job as orderly in the tuberculosis ward that you read about in Chapter Two, Oliver's next job was garbage collector. He rode outside on a big truck and jumped off to pick up and empty the trashcans. He liked it except for one thing: his route included the Cheyenne Mountain Zoo, and he had to pick up after the elephants. That was a stinky job! He later worked as a porter on the passenger train that traveled between Colorado Springs and Sandusky, Ohio. He answered questions the passengers might ask and gave them pillows and blankets if they wanted to take a nap.

After the Civil Rights laws were passed, Oliver was able to go to college and become a teacher. In fact, he went back to Helen Hunt School where he had attended kindergarten through sixth grade and became a well-liked physical education teacher for almost thirty years.

What became of the Green Parrot Shining Parlor on Pikes Peak Avenue? It closed in the fifties, but the building remained and eventually became a Kinko's Copy Shop. In 2008, the building was demolished as part of urban renewal. But in 2001, before the demolition, the manager of Kinko's let Oliver's wife and son go down in the basement. It had hardly changed a bit since that game of "Yokum in the Dark," over fifty years before.

The basement of Green Parrot Shining Parlor.

Photo courtesy of Lucy Bell

Mrs. LeRoy Kirven in front of the Green Parrot Shining Parlor, 214 East
Pikes Peak Avenue, 1940s

Photo courtesy of The Kirven Family

Sixth Grade Class, 1945
Helen Hunt School

The real Oliver with his 6th grade class at Helen Hunt Elementary, 1945

Photo courtesy of Lucy Bell

RESOURCES

General References

Duncan, Fannie Mae and Kathleen F. Esmiol. *Everybody Welcome: A Memoir of Fannie Mae Duncan and the Cotton Club.* Colorado Springs: Chiaroscuro Press, 2013.

McWhorter, John. *Talking Back, Talking Black. Truths About America's Lingua Franca.* New York: Bellevue Literary Press, 2017.

Chapter 1
The Sachs Scholarships for African American Students

Frazier, Effie Evelyn Stroud. "Interview." *Colorado College Oral History Collection.* Colorado Springs: Colorado College, May 30, 1980.

PPLDTV. "The Henry Sachs Foundation." Filmed [1928]. YouTube video, 05:21. Posted [February 13, 2008]. https://www.youtube.com/watch?v=uxWqU1CPWyQ&app=desktop.

Sachs Foundation. "About Us." http://www.sachsfoundation.org (accessed June 28, 2018).

Chapter 2
Tuberculosis Treatment in Colorado Springs

Grimminck, Robert. "10 Ways Tuberculosis Changed the World." March 18, 2015. http://www.toptenz.net/10-ways-tuberculosis-changed-the-world.php (accessed June 28, 2018).

Hunter, Ned. "Halls of History – Sometimes, The Walls Can Talk." *The Gazette (Colorado Springs),* November 24, 2013.

Lewis, Shanna. "How Tuberculosis Fueled Colorado's Growth." *Colorado Public Radio*, February 10, 2015.

Swanson, Mary. "Tuberculosis in Colorado." *Colorado Encyclopedia*, January 14, 2018.

Vail, Nathan. "A Healing Past – Tuberculosis Sanitoriums Were the Springs' 1st Major Economic Driver." *The Gazette (Colorado Springs)*, July 15, 2012.

Chapter 3
Segregation in Colorado Springs

Banks, Charles. "Interview with Charles Banks." Colorado Springs: Pikes Peak Library District, Special Collections, May 18, 1973.

"Negroes To Use Monument Pool Each Wednesday." *Gazette & Telegraph, (Colorado Springs)*, July 21, 1940.

Pollard, Lulu Stroud. "Voices and Visions." Oral History Project of the Colorado Springs Pioneers Museum, December 28, 1993.

Quillen, Ed. "Welcome to Kolorado, Klan Kountry." *Colorado Springs Independent*, May 22, 2003.

Sampson, Ovetta. "A Long Hard Look." *The Gazette (Colorado Springs)*, February 28,1999.

Sprague, Marshall. *One Hundred Plus: A Centennial Story of Colorado Springs*. Colorado Springs Centennial, Inc., 1971.

Stallworth, Ron. *Black Klansman: A Memoir*. New York: Flatiron Books, 2018.

Chapter 4
People's Methodist Episcopal Church

Galloway, Kristine. "Tuskegee Airman Speaks to Cheyenne Students about his Life, Dyslexia." *Wyoming Tribune Eagle,* May 11, 2018.

Holley, John Stokes. *The Invisible People of the Pikes Peak Region: An Afro-American Chronicle.* Colorado Springs: Friends of the Pioneer Museum, 1990.

People's United Methodist Church. *A Brief History of People's United Methodist Church.* Colorado Springs: People's United Methodist Church.

Chapter 5
Job Opportunities Before and After General Palmer's Death

Davant, Jeanne. *Wellsprings: A History of the Pikes Peak Region.* Colorado Springs: Gazette Enterprises, 2001.

Fisher, John S. *A Builder of the West: The Life of General William Jackson Palmer.* Caldwell, ID: Caxton Press, 1939.

Hunter, Samuel C., Sr. "Interview with Samuel C. Hunter, Sr." Colorado Springs: Pikes Peak Library District, Special Collections, June 23, 1973.

NHACS. *Black Settlers of the Pikes Peak Region 1850-1899.* Colorado Springs: Negro Historical Association of Colorado Springs, 1986.

NHACS. *The NHACS Register of Black Settlers in the Pikes Peak Region 1861-1941.* Colorado Springs: Negro Historical Association of Colorado Springs.

NHACS. *1982 Yearbook of the Negro Historical Association of Colorado S Springs*. Colorado Springs: Negro Historical Association of Colorado Springs, 1983.

Stroud, Nina. *The Stroud Family History.* Six-hour DVD set, circa 1990.

LIVING HISTORY

Reflections on Colorado Springs History
By
Franklin James Macon, Documented Original Tuskegee Airman, and grandson of Charles Banks

Franklin Macon struggled with dyslexia while growing up. He has spent the last several years visiting students with dyslexia, inspiring and encouraging them. This photo was taken on May 10, 2018 at Cole Elementary in Cheyenne, Wyoming.

Photo by Jacob Byk/Wyoming Tribune Eagle

Stories of Mrs. Lucy Bell's departed husband, Ollie Bell, bring back both vivid pleasant memories, as well as very unpleasant memories of my childhood in Colorado Springs.

The founder of Colorado Springs, General William J. Palmer was a very open-minded man. He established a superior public school system in Colorado Springs. Thanks to his insight, all children had the opportunity to receive an education from kindergarten to high school, as no school was segregated.

It was after his passing on March 13, 1909, that Colorado Springs suffered a very radical change. The discovery of gold in the Cripple Creek area brought many southern whites to the area, hence they also brought their racially biased attitudes. Colorado Springs was referred to as the "Dixie town" in Colorado.

Not only blacks, but other minorities were affected. Yes, even the poor white population and some religious groups.

Mr. Charles Banks, a Native American, and president of the NAACP at the time of World War II, began a movement to challenge the problem of discrimination in public places. To insure success he selected only people he could trust for this ambitious adventure. These people were his family members.

Numerous lawsuits were brought against businesses and all were fined $500 for a first offence and the fine was doubled for each additional offence.

Thanks to Mr. Charles Banks and family and students of Colorado College as witnesses, the end of discrimination in public places came to an end.

Thank you, Mrs. Lucy Bell, for writing this book.

Historic Note: Franklin, born in 1923, was raised by two great aunts, Maude Gray Macon Loper and Ella Gray Bell, both grandnieces of Frederick Douglass. In 1931, Maude married a prominent black citizen of Colorado Springs named Frank Loper. Loper, who was born a slave on the Jefferson Davis plantation in 1850, became Franklin's step-uncle.

NOTES ON AAVE

Did you notice how the characters in Coming Up spoke? They weren't speaking bad English. They were speaking a different type of English, called African American Vernacular English (AAVE) or Black English. It is different than the Standard English we hear at school and on most television shows.

Black English has different rules for:

- Grammar: the ways words can be put together to make sentences;
- Verb Forms: action words that tell the time that something happened;
- Pronunciation: how words are spoken.

When it comes to speaking Standard English and Black English, never think that one is right and one is wrong; that one is good and one is bad. They are both right and both good. They are just different versions of English.

If you speak both Standard English and AAVE, be proud! Former President Barack Obama is bilingual, too.

If you or your parents would like to learn more about this, read John McWhorter's 2017 book, *Talking Back, Talking Black,* listed in the Resources section.

ACKNOWLEDGMENTS

This book could never have been written without the contributions of many people, who shared conversations and memories that helped bring the stories to life.

Thank you to family members of Oliver Bell: Hazel Bell, sister; Deborah Davis and Joyce Mack, nieces; James and Beverly Bell, cousins.

Thank you to lifelong friends who knew Ollie personally: Reverend Justus Morgan, Sam Dunlap, Reverend Jesse Vaughn, Charles Douglas, and especially Joe Morgan who during our weekly visits, helped me find answers to the many questions that came up about people and events in the book.

Thank you to Colorado Springs residents with family ties to the history of the black community who shared memories and information: Franklin Macon, Esther Holland, Juanita Stroud Martin, Richard and Gwen Walker, Flo Grice Mitchell, Dorothy and Steven Patterson, Manila Green, Sadie Gladden and Leroy Kirven III.

Thank you to all who Assisted with Research: Candice McKnight, President/CEO of AAHGSCS (African-American Historical and Genealogical Society of Colorado Springs) Founder of first black museum in Colorado Springs, 2009; Stephanie Prochaska, Assistant Archivist, Colorado Springs Pioneers Museum; Tim Morris, Special Collections Manager, Pikes Peak Library District. For connecting me to the 1904 Peoples United Methodist Church: Pastor Clifford Seay of the current People's United Methodist Church, his wife and members of his congregation. Pastor Martin Felder, his wife and congregation of Independent Missionary Baptist Church, housed in the 1904 historic building.

Thank you to those who encouraged me to share the "Ollie stories" with the public: Kris Crawford, Vickie Heffner and Dave Rich of the Pillar Institute of Lifelong Learning; Writers Kay Esmiol and Nancy Bentley; Chris Nichol of the Pikes Peak Regional History Symposium; Journalist Bill Vogrin; Peggy Shivers, founder of the Shivers Fund and Concert Series; Great Books facilitator, Christine Hall; Urbanites of the Pikes Peak Region; Adult Forum of First Congregational United Church of Christ; and finally, **My Critique Group** (who read the drafts more times than you would believe:) Mary Ellen Davis, Pat Cook Gulya, Daisy Jackson and Caroline Vulgamore.

CPSIA information can be obtained
at www.ICGtesting.com
Printed in the USA
FSHW02n0701270918
52439FS

9 780986 332456